For Esther and Trini, with love and kisses - S.P-H.

For Eunice, with love and thanks - S.M.

Bloomsbury Publishing, London, Oxford, New York, New Delhi, and Sydney

First published in Great Britain in 2016 by Bloomsbury Publishing Plc
50 Bedford Square, London, WC1B 3DP

Text copyright © Smriti Prasdam-Halls 2016
Illustrations copyright © Sarah Massini 2016
The moral rights of the author and illustrator have been asserted

A CIP catalogue record for this book is available from the British Library

ISBN 978 1 4088 4562 2 (HB)
ISBN 978 1 4088 4563 9 (PB)
ISBN 978 1 4088 4561 5 (eBook)

Printed in China by Leo Paper Products, Heshan, Guangdong

1 3 5 7 9 10 8 6 4 2

All papers used by Bloomsbury Publishing are natural, recyclable products
made from wood grown in well-managed forests.
The manufacturing processes conform to the environmental regulations of the country of origin

www.bloomsbury.com

BLOOMSBURY is a registered trademark of Bloomsbury Publishing Plc

Please return/renew this item by the
last date shown to avoid a charge.
Books may also be renewed by phone
and Internet. May not be renewed if
required by another reader.

www.libraries.barnet.gov.uk

Kiss it Better

Smriti Prasadam-Halls
&
Sarah Massini

BLOOMSBURY
LONDON OXFORD NEW YORK NEW DELHI SYDNEY

Sometimes you feel a bit down in the dumps.
You've scraped your knee,
    you've got bruises and bumps.

Don't worry, a kiss isn't far away . . .

. . . it flies in to find you and saves the day.

A **kiss** for a forehead,

a **kiss** for a nose,

a **kiss** for an elbow,

or **ten wriggly toes**.

It pours out its magic
in each tiny touch,
and tells you each time . . .

"I love you so much."

For did you know **kisses** can actually speak?
Listen the next time one lands on your cheek.

An I'm-sorry kiss helps make amends.

It whispers softly,

"Can we be friends?"

A cheer-up kiss says,
"Tell me what's wrong."

A be-brave kiss
says,
"Come on,
stay strong!"

A see-you-soon kiss
says,

"I'll miss
you, too."

And . . .

. . . a go-to-sleep kiss shouts out,

"MONSTERS, SHOO!"

If thunder storms wake you up with a fright,
a sweet-dreams kiss keeps you safe through the night.

And if you are poorly at home, feeling sick,
grab hold of a get-well-soon kiss – double quick!

Bad moods or accidents,
all first time fears,
grumbles and grouches,
tantrums or tears.

It doesn't matter HOW
funny you feel . . .

Sometimes, it's strange, just **one kiss** will do.
Other times, you'll find you need **quite a few**.

But no matter what your **kisses** are for,
they never run out — there'll always be more!

That's how it works if
you're big and you're tall.

That's how it works
if you're ever so small.

And you'll never guess what — yes, just like you,

sometimes GROWN-UPS need *kisses*, too!

Every day has its ups and its downs.
Sometimes you giggle, sometimes you frown.

But the thing to remember, the secret is this . . .

...EVERYTHING feels better with the help of a

Kiss!